*Zayd, Maliha, and Musa — be rooted in faith, so you
have the courage to follow your dreams.*
– I.M.

*To Rania, in your red coat — your frank kindness fills my heart always.
And to you, reader, who has the superpower to show kindness every day:
may this book help launch the superhero in YOU.*
– S.K.A.

*For my mom, Samia, and my aunt, Mama Samira,
two sisters who hold a special place in my heart.*
– H.A.

Don't miss the bestselling first picture book about Faizah and Asiya,
The Proudest Blue: A Story of Hijab and Family.

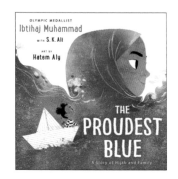

ABOUT THIS BOOK

The illustrations for this book were rendered digitally; the textures were done with ink washes and pencil on watercolour paper. This book was edited by Lisa Yoskowitz and designed by Karina Granda. The production was supervised by Virginia Lawther, and the production editor was Jen Graham. The text was set in Book Antiqua, and the display types are Pinto and Lunchbox.

First published in Great Britain in 2023 by Andersen Press Ltd., 20 Vauxhall Bridge Road, London SW1V 2SA • Vijverlaan 48, 3062 HL Rotterdam, Nederland • Text copyright © 2023 by Ibtihaj Muhammad • Illustrations copyright © 2023 by Hatem Aly • Author photo on page 34 courtesy of Ibtihaj Muhammad • Published by arrangement with Hachette Book Group, 1290 Avenue of the Americas, New York, NY 10104 • The rights of Ibtihaj Muhammad and Hatem Aly to be identified as author and illustrator of this work have been asserted by them in accordance with the Copyright, Designs and Patents Act, 1988 All rights reserved • Printed and bound in Spain • British Library Cataloguing in Publication Data available • HARDBACK ISBN 978 1 83913 303 9 • PAPERBACK ISBN 978 1 83913 304 6 • 10 9 8 7 6 5 4 3 2 1

THE KINDEST RED

A Story of Hijab and Friendship

Ibtihaj Muhammad

and S. K. Ali · Art by Hatem Aly

Ⓐ

ANDERSEN PRESS

MAMA HOLDS UP THE DRESS.

My sister Asiya's dress.
Before that, Mama's dress.
Now it's mine.

I hug it close.

I've been waiting so
long to wear it.

Asiya does my hair.
Just like Mama taught her.

She says, "Almost done, Faizah."
Just like Mama.

I get to slide the sparkliest scarf pin into Asiya's hijab to hug it tight.

Mama takes our Picture Day picture before waving goodbye. "My kind, beautiful girls. Remember, you are strong and smart. You can do and be anything!"

At school, my friend Sophie twirls in a dress with big red roses.
And the biggest red sash.

I twirl to show her we match.
We march into class together.

"Today is a special day! It's time to think about what kind of world we want to live in," Ms Ramirez says. "What kind of world do *you* want?"

She writes *all* of our answers on the board.

* ICE CREAM WORLD
* SUNNY WORLD
* HAPPY WORLD
* HEALTHY WORLD
* FUNNY WORLD
* FAIR WORLD
* SWEET WORLD
* UNICORN WORLD

It's going to be such a good world!

Ms Ramirez asks each of us to draw the world we want and give it a name.

Everyone around me picks up their coloured pencils.
I see Sophie drawing superheroes, lightning bolts and flowers.

Mama would say: *Draw a beautiful world.*

Asiya would say: *Draw a strong world.*

What do I want?

A kind world.

A world where there's always a friend nearby.

A world of friends helping one another.

"Okay, class, it's break time," Ms Ramirez says. "Are you ready to make your wishes for the world come true?"

When we get outside, I link my arm with Sophie's.

"Let's make the world kinder," I say.
"With our superpowers!" Sophie says.

We look for ways to grow a kind-powered world.

Mali wants someone to bounce a ball with.

Andre wants to play with London, so we look for her.

Jada wants to play tag, so we chase each other.

It's going to be such a
good world!

At lunchtime, our class keeps using our
powers to make the best world.

I run to Asiya to make *her* day even better, and ask her,
"Is there anything I can help you with?"

She smiles and gives me and Sophie and Jada a turn with her basketball.

We feel even more powerful after that.

Priya needs help putting a plaster on her hand.

Sophie needs her sash tied into a big bow.

Mateo needs help with his bowtie.

Sophie needs her sash tied into a big bow, again.

Violet and Felix need to stop fighting over the skipping-rope, so they decide to take turns.

When it's time to line up, Sophie needs her sash tied into a big bow *again*.

Mateo and I help her.

Our class picture is full of big smiles.

Later, Asiya comes to pick me up from my classroom.
Sophie's brother and Priya's sisters come to pick them up too.
It's sibling picture time!
Me and Asiya, all by ourselves!

We join the queue. Mali is wearing the same shirt as her siblings.

Andre has the same tie as his brother.

Priya is wearing jeans like her sisters.

Sophie's brother even has a vest covered with roses.

Seeing them makes me happy *and* sad.

Because Asiya and I don't match.

AT ALL.

When Sophie sees my face, she asks, "Are you okay?"
Jada asks, "Do you need help?"

I tell them.

Jada says something to Sophie, and Sophie nods
and pulls her sash so hard its big bow falls.

She pulls it out of its loops, and Jada spreads it out,
and it's big and wide and strong … just like …

Asiya's hijab.

It's the most beautiful
Picture Day ever.

Just like Mama wanted.

I want a kind world.
A world where kindness passes from one to another.

Like Mama passing
on her dress.

Like Asiya doing
my hair.

Like our class passing power to each other.

Like Jada passing
on an idea.

And Sophie
passing her sash.

Like me passing
on this story.

AUTHOR'S NOTE

Dear Reader,

My parents would often dress me and my sisters in matching outfits when we were kids – from the beads in our braided hair to our kente cloth dresses. We shared things like hijabs and hair ties and understood that the dresses of an older sister would eventually become our own.

That's the thing about family: kindness is woven into its fabric. Whether it's sharing a snack or advice, an everyday act of kindness can be big or small. Faith teaches us that kindness is an important part of life. It serves as a beautiful reminder of how our own behaviour can affect those around us.

While my sisters and I are now all grown up, the memories of the good times that we shared, and even the matching outfits, will always be with me. This book is a celebration of family and the joy of helping others. May you always know that joy.

Brandilyn (sister, age 8), Qareeb (brother, age 3), and Ibtihaj (age 2)